MIA MAYHEM

3 BOOKS IN 1!

MIA MAYHEM IS A SUPERHERO!

MIA MAYHEM LEARNS TO FLY!

MIA MAYHEM VS. THE SUPER BULLY

BY **KARA WEST**   ILLUSTRATED BY **LEEZA HERNANDEZ**

P9-CBW-524

LITTLE SIMON

New York   London   Toronto   Sydney   New Delhi

LITTLE SIMON

An imprint of Simon & Schuster Children's Publishing Division

New York London Toronto Sydney New Delhi

1230 Avenue of the Americas, New York, New York 10020

Mia Mayhem Is a Superhero! and *Mia Mayhem Learns to Fly!* copyright © 2018
by Simon & Schuster, Inc.

Mia Mayhem vs. the Super Bully as copyright © 2019
by Simon & Schuster, Inc.

This Little Simon bind-up edition May 2022

For information about special discounts for bulk purchases, please contact
Simon & Schuster Special Sales at 1-866-506-1949 or business@simonandschuster.com.
The Simon & Schuster Speakers Bureau can bring authors to your live event. For more
information or to book an event contact the Simon & Schuster Speakers Bureau at
1-866-248-3049 or visit our website at www.simonspeakers.com.
Series design by Laura Roode
Manufactured in the United States of America 0322 MTN
2 4 6 8 10 9 7 5 3 1
Library of Congress Control Number 2021952205
ISBN 978-1-6659-1902-9
ISBN 978-1-5344-3271-0 (*Mia Mayhem Is a Superhero!* ebook)
ISBN 978-1-5344-3274-1 (*Mia Mayhem Learns to Fly!* ebook)
ISBN 978-1-5344-4475-1 (*Mia Mayhem vs. the Super Bully* ebook)
These titles were previously published individually
in hardcover and paperback by Little Simon.

MIA MAYHEM
IS A SUPERHERO!
PAGE 4

MIA MAYHEM
LEARNS TO FLY!
PAGE 128

MIA MAYHEM
VS. THE SUPER BULLY
PAGE 250

IS A SUPERHERO!

CONTENTS

THE UNEXPECTED LETTER

Okay, I know this doesn't look good. It definitely seems like a tornado just blew through my house. I spilled a whole bag of flour, broke a window, ran through the screen door, was licked by a bunch of dogs, and even got my shoe stuck in a tree.

But I have an excuse. Really, I do.

It's been a *super*-exciting day.

Seriously *super*. Why?

Well, hold on to your socks. . . .

Here's the deal:

You ready?

I. Mia Macarooney. Am. A. Superhero!

For. *Real*. Yours truly has superpowers!

And believe it or not, I *just* found out myself. In fact, my life was completely ordinary . . . until this afternoon.

I had a normal, uneventful day at school, and my best friend, Eddie, and I walked home, just like every other

8

single day ever. At my driveway, I checked the mailbox like I always did. Except today, there was a tattered letter covered in stamps . . . addressed to me!

It said:

DEAR MISS MIA MACAROONEY,

CONGRATULATIONS! WE'RE VERY PLEASED TO INFORM YOU OF YOUR ACCEPTANCE TO THE PROGRAM FOR IN TRAINING SUPERHEROES (THE PITS). I LOOK FORWARD TO MEETING YOU AT YOUR FIRST SUPERHERO-TRAINING SESSION!

BEST WISHES,

Dr. Sue Perb

HEADMISTRESS

Uhh . . . *the program for in training what?* This couldn't be real.

I wasn't *super*. How could I be? I don't have superpowers! I'd definitely know if I did, right? Plus, I have a bit of a reputation for causing chaos and mayhem wherever I go.

I never mean to . . . but the truth is, I'm a total disaster-machine! Like one time I kicked a soccer ball that broke a steel goalpost in half. Another time, I flooded the hallways after using the water fountain.

So, you see what I mean? This couldn't be real.

I flipped over the letter to see if it said "GOTCHA!" on the back.

Nope. Nothing.

So I ran inside and triple-checked.

"You read that right. It's true, honey!" my mom exclaimed when I showed her the letter. "We've been waiting *forever*. We went to the PITS too!"

I looked up at her in total shock.

"This letter sure traveled a long way. We're thrilled for you, honey! You won't be *too* far behind," she said.

"Behind?" I asked.

"Well, you see, most kids start their training in kindergarten," Dad said.

I grabbed the piece of paper and read it again.

"No way! My letter is three years late?" I exclaimed.

"Don't worry, honey. You'll catch up as fast as lightning!" my dad said with a wink.

So just like that, I got the biggest, most unbelievable, best news ever! Can you believe it? All this time I thought I was a super-klutz . . . but turns out, I'm just *super*! *And* I always *have* been!

My
Superfamily

"You might want to sit down for this," Mom said with a huge grin on her face.

I nervously backed into a chair as my cat, Chaos, jumped onto my lap.

"We're so happy we can finally tell you the Macarooney super-secret," Mom began slowly. "We're a family of superheroes!"

My jaw dropped to the floor.

"No way! So you're not really a flight attendant?" I asked.

"Of course I am!" she said, "But truth is, I can fly without a plane."

Okay, hold on. Did you just hear that?

This day has officially gone from really normal to really cool *super*fast.

"Wait a minute! Then are you really a veterinarian?" I asked my dad.

"Sure am! And I can talk to animals, too," he said. "Here, let me show you."

My dad looked straight into Chaos's eyes and started *meowing* . . . just like her!

MEOW, ME ME, MEOW!

WHEEEEE!

And believe it or not, my cat stood up and did a triple backflip onto the ground!

"Atta girl!" my dad said as they fist-bumped each other.

I sat back in shock, trying to take it all in. I couldn't believe it. I still had *so* many questions. But here's what I just learned: My cat is *way* smarter than I thought, my parents are real *superheroes* . . . and SO. AM. I!

"This is AWESOME!" I finally yelled out.

"Oh, Mia. We're thrilled for you!" my mom exclaimed. "We have to celebrate!"

"I know we already made cookies, but this news calls for more dessert!" my dad said.

I nodded excitedly. My dad always had good ideas.

POOF!

Well, it *was* a good idea . . . until I plopped the bag of flour down on the counter. *POOF!*

Flour got all over my face and even up my nose! Then Chaos started to run in circles, making the mess EVEN BIGGER!

I tried *really* hard to ignore the tickle in my nose, which turned out to be another not-so-good idea . . . because I sneezed so loudly that the big kitchen window CRACKED!

I swear I didn't mean to make things worse.

But it was too late. The noise made Chaos run off in an absolute frenzy.

I quickly wiped my eyes and ran after her. But as I rounded the corner, I tripped and fell . . . and my sneaky cat ran off with my shoe!

So obviously, I chased after her as fast as I could.

The only problem is, my top speed is a little *too* fast, even in crazy cat emergencies like this, because I tore through the screen door . . . and now there's a giant hole in it as big as me!

CHAPTER 3

STUCK UP
A TREE

Whoops!

I swear I didn't mean to burst through the door.

But believe it or not, I'm pretty used to craziness like this. Me and my cat both are! That's why I named her Chaos. She just *loves* messes!

And unfortunately for me, she's also *really good* at running away.

"Chaos! Where are you?" I hollered as I looked around my backyard.

I kept yelling until I heard a soft cry. From all the way up a tree!

"Chaos! What are you doing up there?" I exclaimed. I could tell by the look in her eyes that she couldn't get down. I started pacing back and forth nervously.

You see, I know I can climb up . . . because I *am* pretty strong. The only problem is, I absolutely hate heights. So I stood still, thinking *really hard* about what to do, when all of a sudden, there was a loud noise.

Oh no! Did I somehow break the fence just by *thinking*?

I know it sounds crazy. But now that I'm a SUPERHERO, anything can happen, right?

I held my breath, expecting the fence to break. But instead, a pack of dogs bounded over, circled me, and started barking.

I froze with my hands over my ears until I heard someone call my name.

"Don't worry, Mia! They won't hurt you," my dad exclaimed. "They heard Chaos's cry and came over to warn me!"

Then my dad ran over and started *barking* at the dogs. Every single one of them immediately calmed down.

"Ah, that's better," Dad said with a grin.

ARF!

ARF!

YIP!

YIP!

"And don't worry, Chaos!" Mom exclaimed. "I'll be right there!"

My mom then flew into the air as my jaw dropped to the ground.

Whoa. Did you just see that? MY MOM CAN *REALLY* FLY!

When she landed with Chaos safely in her arms, I ran over and gave them a huge hug.

I can't believe my parents just saved the day!

CHAPTER
4

LIVING IN A NORMAL WORLD

"Wow, I'm sorry. I really didn't mean to . . . ," I began as we walked back into the house.

"It's okay, Mia. I'm just glad you and Chaos are safe," my mom replied.

"And luckily, we have some extra help!" Dad said, pointing to the dogs.

Wait, hold on. Did I just *not* get into trouble?

That's not what
I was expecting . . .
but I could definitely
get used to
this!

My dad
then gave each
dog a job. They immediately started
cleaning food, books, and cushions off
the ground.

"This is amazing!" I cried.
"With your powers, this mess
will be gone in a flash!"
"Oh, Mia, you'll
learn all kinds of

super-skills at the PITS," Mom said with a smile. "But it's important to know that with great power comes great responsibility."

"Like protecting you and saving Chaos, for example," Dad continued. "That's what superheroes do!"

"But since we live in a normal world, we also have to protect ourselves," Mom explained,  "by maintaining our secret identities."

"That's why we hold everyday jobs, why you will still go to your regular school, and why we do *most* things the old-fashioned way . . . with a few special exceptions," Dad added with a wink.

Then he turned to the hole in the screen door and shot lasers *out of his hands*! And just like that it was repaired.

45

"Wow. That's awesome!" I exclaimed as I grabbed a regular old broom.

Luckily, even without any special help, we finished cleaning in no time. Then we made brownies by hand, just like we had planned.

But as I was washing up, I realized there was just one tiny problem.

"Mom, how am I supposed to keep this super-secret from everyone?" I asked.

"Oh, don't worry. You can't possibly keep it a secret from *everyone*," Mom replied. "Even superheroes need people they can trust."

"Oh thank goodness!" I exclaimed.

This was great news . . . because I am absolutely *terrible* at keeping secrets. Especially from Eddie.

So as soon as the oven beeped, I grabbed some brownies, shoved the acceptance letter into my pocket, and ran out the door.

PURR!

PURR!

CHAPTER 5

SPILLING THE BEANS

"These brownies look delicious, Mia!" Eddie's mom exclaimed when she opened the door.

"Oh yes! They're yummy, Mrs. Stein!" I replied as I gave her one.

Then I ran to Eddie's room and burst open the door. I may have pushed a little *too* hard though because a gust of wind blew through the room!

I lifted my hand to make it stop. And thankfully, it worked! The wind calmed down. The only problem was, *everything else* froze too!

Oh man. I have no idea what I just did. But see that kid over there? The one who looks totally surprised? His name is Edison Stein, or Eddie for short, and he's my best friend.

He's *super*smart. And he always has my back. Even when I cause mayhem. In fact, remember how I broke the goalpost? Well, Eddie was the goalie. And he told our coach that the post was already broken . . . and our coach believed it!

So I'm hoping Eddie won't be *too* mad about this. It looks like he's busy working on something *super*-important.

All I need to do is figure out how to unfreeze him.

"Umm . . .  melt!" I commanded.

Nothing.

"Undo!"

Nope.

"Simon says?" I tried.

After a dozen commands, I gave up and reached my hand out in front of me.

And that actually worked!

"Uh, Mia?" Eddie called out. "Is that you?"

"Sorry! I got a little *too* excited," I replied.

"To bring me brownies?" he asked doubtfully as he grabbed one.

"Oh yeah, these brownies are so good," I replied as I took a deep breath. "But I've got something to tell you . . . and you have to *promise* you won't tell a soul."

So we did our secret handshake.

"Okay. This is crazy, but . . . I just found out that I'm not a super-klutz. I'm actually *super*!"

"Of course you are. You're great!" Eddie replied.

"No, like for real! I just found out I have . . . superpowers!"

He took a bite of his brownie and looked at me, clearly confused.

"Here, I have proof," I continued, pulling out the letter.

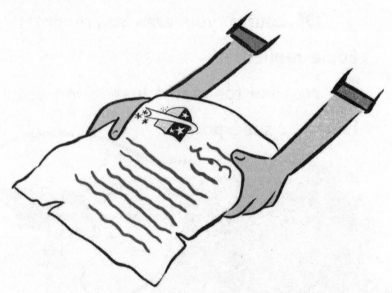

I filled him in on the mess that I made at my house, and then I waited patiently.

He flipped over the paper just like I had and read it again.

Still nothing. So I waited some more.

Then, after what felt like *forever*, he looked up at me with the biggest smile I've ever seen.

WELCOME TO THE PITS!

The next day, after the longest English class ever, my parents came to pick me up early. We were going to the PITS together for the first time . . . and I couldn't wait!

When we finally left, I expected to see a jet. Or a hovercraft. Or even a submarine! Because after all, we were going to a top secret superhero training academy, so it would only make sense to arrive in style, right?

So obviously, I couldn't believe it when we simply walked to an empty, abandoned warehouse . . . that was right next to my school!

"Umm . . . is the jet inside here?" I asked.

"The *what*?" my mom asked with a laugh. "No, honey. We're here!"

Wait. This must be a mistake. Are you seeing what I'm seeing?

This is an empty warehouse. This can't possibly be it!

There's even a crooked DO NOT ENTER sign dangling on the side.

I was about to tell her that we were *definitely* in the wrong place, when she reached out and straightened the sign.

Then guess what happened?

The concrete bricks *shifted* around . . . until a hidden screen popped up!

My parents knew exactly what to do. My mom and dad stood still. Then they opened their eyes wide as a red light carefully scanned their faces.

When the light turned green, a secret entrance appeared . . . out of nowhere!

A tall, elegant woman in a sleek, black skintight suit was waiting for us as soon as we walked in.

"Ah, it's so great to see you!" she said as she gave my parents a hug.

"Oh wow, and you must be Mia!" she exclaimed happily. "Welcome to the PITS! My name is Dr. Sue Perb."

When we arrived at the main lobby, I couldn't believe my eyes! From the outside this building looked like a boring, old warehouse. But on the inside, there were floor-to-ceiling windows and huge forty-foot-tall screens everywhere!

"Welcome to the Compass!" Dr. Perb exclaimed. "If you ever get lost, all you need to do is come back to the heart of the PITS."

I looked around in awe as we stood in the middle of a gigantic compass that was in the marble floor.

The crazy thing is, this wasn't even the coolest part!

Because there were actual real-life *superheroes* everywhere!

Dr. Perb must have seen my mouth hanging open because she turned to me and said, "It's a lot to take in, isn't it? We have the best superheroes teaching here. You're in good hands, Mia."

Wait. Did you hear that? That man with the winged suit is going to be my teacher!

And just when I thought things couldn't get *any* cooler, she led us into the fanciest headmistress's office EVER.

"First, we need to scan and secure your identity," Dr. Sue Perb said as she offered us seats. "So that you can enter the building!"

She typed away on her computer as a drone camera scanned my entire body.

"You are now in the PITS Superhero Database!" she exclaimed minutes later. "You will get a full tour tomorrow, but I called you in before any students arrive because today is the first and last day you will come as Mia Macarooney.

Starting tomorrow, you are to come in your supersuit. You'll also be registered into our database under your very own superhero name! It's our top priority to protect your secret identity."

"But . . . I don't have a supersuit *or* a name!" I replied.

"Don't worry. We're going to take care of the supersuit," she said. "But your superhero name is up to you. You'll know exactly when you find it . . . but until then, simply going as 'Mia' is just fine."

Then she pulled a green leaf on her desk plant, and she spoke into it.

"Professor Stu Pendus, please come in."

A wall panel opened up, and a man burst out, shimmering in green.

"Mia, meet Professor Stu Pendus! He's the mastermind behind everyone's supersuit . . . including yours!"

Professor Stu Pendus led me into a huge room stocked with colorful fabrics, took my measurements, and started pulling things off the shelf.

A lot of them were *super*crazy.

And weird.

And totally

not me.

Until finally, we found it:

the perfect suit.

THE TOUR

At school the next day, the morning passed by *incredibly* slowly. I was so nervous that I couldn't sit still! But can you blame me? Today was my first day at the PITS, and I couldn't wait to meet other superheroes just like me!

I tapped my pencil on my desk as I watched the clock. When the bell rang, I jumped up as Eddie came over.

It was going to be weird not going home together, but I promised to tell him all about it.

Then I rushed into the bathroom to change . . . into my very own suit! But I'll definitely have to work on the quick-superhero-change thing . . . because before I knew it, I was running late!

Once I
arrived at
the warehouse,
I adjusted the
DO NOT ENTER
sign.

But nothing happened.

So I twirled it.
Pulled it.
Pushed it.
Still nothing.

I stood there totally confused till someone tapped me on the shoulder.

"It only works at a specific angle," a boy wearing a blazing red cape explained.

He tilted the sign and the screen appeared. I watched him as he scanned his face.

Then it was my turn. I did exactly as he did . . . and thankfully, it worked!

Dr. Sue Perb was waiting for me inside. "Ah, you two have already met!" she exclaimed. "Penn Powers, could you please show Mia around before her placement exam? You'll probably be in

some of the same classes. Today is her very first day."

"What? There's an exam?" I cried.

"Don't freak out. It's not a big deal. You can't study for it," Penn Powers replied rather coolly.

"He's right, Mia. There's nothing to worry about! Please enjoy your tour!"

Dr. Sue Perb exclaimed. I thanked her and then ran to catch up with Penn, who had already walked away.

Luckily, the nerves about the exam went away as we passed by classrooms for flying, strength training, superspeed, and my dad's special power . . . talking to animals.

"The building has five identical floors with hallways that all lead back to the Compass. Each wing of the PITS is dedicated to a specific superfield of study," Penn explained. "Beginner-level classes are on the first floor, and grand-master studies are at the top."

I listened very carefully, trying to take it all in.

"Wow, those kids are really flying!" I exclaimed as I peeked in to one of the rooms.

"Actually, they're learning how to jump. It's the most basic skill of flying," Penn replied matter-of-factly.

"When will I learn to do that?" I asked excitedly.

"Well, obviously, you'll find out after your exam. Until then, just come with me—I'm late for flying class!"

CHAPTER 8

PROFESSOR WINGUM'S FLYING CLASS

"What's on the third floor?" I asked as we rushed into a glass elevator.

"All advanced courses," he replied. "Most kids our age are on the second floor, in junior-level classes . . . but I'm a *super*-flier!"

Wow!

Did you hear that?

He must be really talented.

Okay, I'll be honest. Up until right now, I felt good about being a newbie superhero. After all, there's something that feels *super*-right about being with other kids . . . just like me! But now, I'm starting to feel pretty out of place.

When the elevator doors opened, I gasped for the hundredth time.

We were standing in front of the coolest obstacle course EVER! There was an awesome rock-climbing wall, a moving jungle gym, tightropes, and even floating monkey bars!

And guess what?

The same man in the winged suit from yesterday came flying toward us.

WHOOSH!

"Hello! You must be Mia. Dr. Sue Perb told me that Penn was taking you around," he said warmly. "My name is Professor Wingum."

As he landed to shake my hand, Penn flew off to join the rest of the kids.

I watched in awe as Penn dove through hoops, spun around poles, and glided above the water.

"Not bad, eh?" Professor Wingum
asked proudly. "Penn is a natural."
I nodded my head in disbelief.

"I know you're taking your placement exam after this, but would you like to hop on the ropes?" Professor Wingum asked. "It'll help you get used to heights."

Now, watching Penn fly around must have made me feel *super*brave . . . because I surprisingly said yes.

I jumped onto the rope as Dr. Wingum spotted me from behind. And at first, going up was a piece of cake!

But I should have never looked down. Why?

Well, do you see that? Look at how high I am!

Worst. Idea. Ever.

Thankfully, though, it reminded me of the time I got stuck at the top of a Ferris wheel.

And I remembered what had calmed me down before.

Inhale.

Exhale.

Inhale.

Exhale.

In—

Are you wondering what that sound was?

Oh, don't worry. It's just the sound
of . . . THE ROPE BREAKING!

I yelled out at the top of my lungs
as I frantically swung back and forth.
I hoped my loud shrieking would get
someone's attention, but it was no use.

I was about to fall twenty feet . . . and NO ONE COULD HEAR ME!

I shut my eyes and braced myself for the worst. A horrible, nauseating feeling in my stomach grew bigger and bigger . . . until suddenly, like magic, it disappeared!

Someone had come to the rescue!

I relaxed as we flew around in a circle. I was even enjoying the ride . . . until I opened my eyes.

I couldn't believe I was being carried to safety by . . . Penn Powers!

How embarrassing!

And unfortunately, things got even more awkward. Because when we landed, my legs totally gave out and Penn helped me up . . . *again*!

Then he proudly took a bow as everyone burst into applause.

CHAPTER 9

THE WEIRDEST TEST EVER

Ugh. Are you kidding me?

No one told me these ropes were part of the exam!

I'm stuck here again. And there's no way I'm moving. Not even one inch.

I seriously can't believe I have to do this *again* after what I just went through in Professor Wingum's class.

This superhero business is no joke.

And it doesn't help that being stuck here is just as embarrassing as before . . . but embarrassing or not, I don't think flying is my thing.

So obviously, I did the same thing I did earlier: yell for mercy!

This time, Professor Dina Myte, Dr. Sue Perb's second in command, got me down . . . instead of Penn.

Being saved wasn't fun, but I hoped I'd

have better luck at talking to animals because after all . . . I had a cat!

Unfortunately, this wasn't the case. Because I somehow managed to offend a dog, confuse a bird, and put a newt to sleep!

zzZ Z

Now, before I go on, let me just say that yes, I was disappointed to know that I was not very good at *either* of my parents' skills.

But if my mom and dad have something special, I must have one too, right?

Well, I wish I could tell you that I found it. But . . . I didn't. And things just got weirder. Because during the strength-training portion, I had to lift an elephant *and* a car!

Then for superspeed, I fumbled my way through an obstacle course with a million hurdles!

After that, I had to try to make four pencils float in midair, freeze and unfreeze water droplets, and even try to shoot lasers out of my eyes!

Can you guess how it all went?

Yep, that's right. Not well. At all.

By the end of the last skill test, I was pooped.

And believe it or not, that wasn't even all of it!

"It's time for the written portion now!" Professor Myte exclaimed as she handed me a stack of papers.

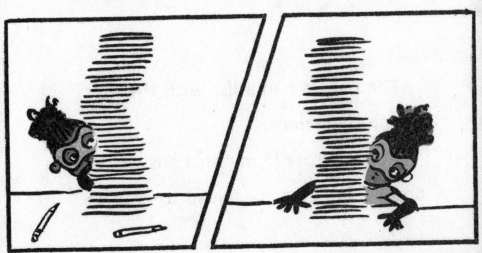

TEST

1. What's your best dance move?

2. Favorite ice-cream flavor?

3. Can you touch your nose with your tongue?

4. Have you ever been seasick?

The papers had a list with the most random questions.

After I wrote in my final answer, the longest day ever continued to drag on.

CHAPTER 10

MAYHEM ARRIVES!

"How was your first day?" Dr. Sue Perb asked as I nervously walked into her office.

I looked down at my feet. Was I supposed to tell her how embarrassing and disastrous it was? Did she know that I got stuck on the ropes *twice* and was even saved by Penn Powers?

In the end I told her the truth.

"This place is *super*cool . . . but to be honest I'm not sure I'm cut out for this," I mumbled, trying not to cry.

"Oh, Mia. Every superhero is born with special powers, but becoming a *real* superhero takes work," she said warmly. "Believe it or not, superheroes aren't made overnight."

Then she handed me a piece of paper.

"Congratulations!" she exclaimed. "You're at the junior level for everything . . . except flying and foreign languages. You'll be in beginner-level classes for those." She gave me a pat on the back as I looked at her in shock.

I grabbed the paper and looked closely.

How was this possible? I was so sure I'd failed!

"Is this for real?" I asked.

"Of course it is!" Dr. Sue Perb exclaimed. "Our exam is completely foolproof. Every training schedule is tailored to each student."

Then she reached out from under her desk and handed me my favorite ice cream!

I must have looked confused because she asked, "What did you think the written exam was for? We just wanted to get to know you better!"

At that, I couldn't help but laugh. Ice cream always made everything better.

"Learning to control all your powers will take time," she went on. "But trust me, Mia. You'll learn how to embrace any chaos and mayhem that's bound to come with it."

I nodded, with a big smile across my face.

I *definitely* had a lot to learn . . . but at least I knew I wasn't alone.

"Now, I know it's been an extremely long day, but there's one last step to becoming an official PITS superhero," Dr. Sue Perb said. "A student photo!"

"Okay, Mia. Are you ready? Give me your best superhero pose!" Professor Stu Pendus exclaimed.

After a bunch of different shots, I ran out of ideas. So finally, I just put my hands on my hips.

"Great, Mia! That's the one! Now hold it," Professor Stu Pendus said.

I smiled big and leaned back . . . but turns out, that wasn't the best idea.

"OH NO!" I yelled, reaching my hand out.

Everything instantly froze. Just like at Eddie's house.

Whoa, I still have no idea how I did that. But thank goodness!

I grabbed the light stand and put it back on the floor.

CRASH!

Phew. Okay, before anything else crazy happens, let's recap: I just had the weirdest, most unbelievable week . . . EVER! It was good; it was bad and full of mayhem. But you know what? I'm starting to believe that a little mayhem is okay. Because it turns out all those times I thought I was a total disaster-machine—like when I broke the goalpost or flooded the school hallways—I was actually using my superpowers. I just didn't know it!

And that's why from now on, you can call me Mia Mayhem. I'm the world's newest superhero!

127

LEARNS TO FLY!

CONTENTS

CHAPTER 1

IN THE DOGHOUSE

Most cats like to lay in the sun or scratch at things or take naps.

But not *my* cat: Chaos is her name, and chaos is her game. On a typical afternoon, she'll excitedly zoom around the kitchen, knock over a honey bottle, and then land right in the middle of it.

And as you can see, that's exactly what just happened.

Chaos doesn't really *mean* to cause trouble. And I should know. I have a bit of a reputation for causing chaos and mayhem myself.

Oh, I should probably explain before I go on. Allow me to introduce myself. My name is Mia Macarooney.

During the day, I attend Normal Elementary School. But as soon as the school bell rings, I'm Mia Mayhem—the world's newest superhero!

For real. Yours truly has superpowers!

And guess what? I'm going to learn how to *fly!*

BRRIIING!

And that means when regular school ends, I head straight to the Program for In Training Superheroes aka the PITS! But today, my flying class was starting late, so I ran home to make a honey and peanut butter sandwich.

Sounds like a great idea, right?

I thought so too. But as you can see, things can get pretty sticky real fast if you have a curious cat like mine.

I may have superpowers, but cleaning a whole jar of honey off a crazy cat? That's a job for a professional.

So I rushed Chaos over to my dad's animal clinic.

He's really good with animals. And I don't just mean as a veterinarian.

Here's the deal: He's a superhero too! Both my parents are.

Just like me, my mom and dad lead ordinary lives in order to protect their secret identities. Most of the time, our lives are pretty quiet. But turns out today was not the best time for a vet visit. The office was busy because the Downtown Dog Palooza, our town's annual dog show, was tomorrow.

I nervously looked at the clock. I was going to be late for class. But luckily, my dad cleaned up Chaos in a flash.

I led my cat back into her carrier and sped out the door without looking back. I had to get to the PITS before the last bell.

Thankfully, I didn't have to go too far because the PITS building was right next to my regular school! All my life, I thought it was just an empty warehouse . . . but everything changed when I found out I was a *superhero*!

Turns out that this normal old warehouse is the coolest place *ever*! (But more on that later.)

When I arrived at the front entrance, I grabbed my supersuit from my bag and spun around.

This new quick-superhero-change trick took *a lot* of practice. I held out my hand to Chaos for a fist bump, but when I looked down . . . Chaos wasn't the only animal there!

There was a pack of dogs excitedly panting all around me. Somehow we'd been followed! I instantly regretted not making sure the door was closed after leaving the clinic.

I looked around nervously. There was only one I recognized—my best friend's dog, Pax.

WOOF! Pax jumped on me so hard that I fell back.

When I picked myself up, that's
when I heard it.

Someone was coming, and I had to
think fast . . . or we would all be seen!

I quickly straightened
the crooked DO NOT ENTER
sign—which opened
the secret entrance
to the PITS—and
scanned myself in.

As the door opened, Chaos pawed her way out of the carrier and raced into the building—with the pack of dogs right behind her!

Oh boy. I was in the doghouse now.

145

CHAPTER 2

THE WIND TUNNEL

I chased after Chaos and the dogs into the main lobby. The center of the tall building, also known as the Compass, was bustling with superheroes. I thought that I'd get in trouble for bringing in a pack of loose animals, but no one stopped us!

I think that's because everyone here has seen weirder things.

The PITS is a top secret superhero-training academy that offers classes in every super-skill, from flying to foreign languages. (That's the class where you learn how to talk to animals.)

And look—I almost crashed into someone who was shooting heat lasers into a wall. This place is the coolest!

So I guess seeing a pack of adorable dogs chasing a speedy cat is . . . actually normal.

When I finally got to Professor Wingum's flying class, he didn't ask any questions or even get angry!

149

"Ah, Mia, you're here!" he said with a smile. "Please join us. I don't mind watching your furry friends."

I thanked him and let out a huge sigh of relief. Then I ran over to my classmates.

"Everyone, welcome to Flying 101!" Professor Wingum said as he scratched a big black Great Dane behind the ears. "Today's lesson is the wind tunnel."

In the center of the room was a long, clear glass cylinder with a steel frame. Professor Wingum walked over to it and pushed a round white button on the control panel. The vents at the top, bottom, and sides of the tunnel instantly turned on.

"Your mission is to fly against the wind. This helps build core strength," Professor Wingum began. "Since this is a beginner-level class, there are no obstacles. But it *is* timed. If you take too long, an alarm will go off. The key is to stay focused and balanced while keeping a steady speed."

I looked around to see if any of my peers looked as nervous as me.

Now, I know flying *sounds* really cool, but it's actually *way* harder than it looks. In my first flying class ever, I was saved by . . . that kid!

"Class, please say hi to Penn Powers!" Professor Wingum announced excitedly. "He'll be showing us how it's done."

I immediately hid behind the tallest
kid in class. The last time I had seen
Penn, I was stuck on a really long rope.
It was *super*-embarrassing.

Penn Powers walked into the tunnel. Everyone watched in awe as he easily flew against the powerful wind. He even did a bunch of fancy flips!

When he came out, he bowed as kids burst into applause.

After that I was glad I was going last. Maybe my nerves would calm down before it was my turn.

Some kids had a hard time and other kids did okay, but no one flew as well as Penn. Soon, it was  my turn. I stepped into the tunnel, and my stomach dropped to the floor. I took a deep breath and closed my eyes. Then I bent down to push off—when suddenly, I felt something soft brush against my leg.

"Chaos!" I yelled as my cat was swept into the wind tunnel. Without thinking, I jumped in after her.

As we tumbled through the air, I wondered if this day could get any worse. And then it did.

Because *all* the dogs jumped in too!

CHAPTER
3

PAWSITIVELY HEROIC

So there I was. Trapped in a giant wind tunnel, rolling around with my crazy cat and a pack of adorable dogs.

This was not one of my best moments—that was for sure.

But turns out that there *was* one good thing about all this. Looking at Chaos's scaredy-cat face, I realized that it was up to me to save the day.

I held my arms out in front of me and leaned forward as hard as I could. And it totally worked!

I flew toward Chaos, and before I knew it I was so close that I could almost touch her.

But then someone else grabbed her!

I looked up and saw Penn Powers, holding my cat.

And the thing is, he wasn't just holding Chaos. I watched as Penn started gathering all the floating dogs, too.

He put a bunch of dogs on his back
as he held more in his arms. I could tell
it was too much. Even for him.

"Hey, Penn! Let me help!" I yelled. I may not be great at flying yet, but I knew I was strong. After all, during my PITS placement test, I lifted an elephant *and* a car!

"No, I got it!" he replied. "Just make sure to fly through the exit before your timer goes off!"

"Penn, this is too much weight to handle by yourself!" I tried again.

But he just waved me on and grabbed another dog . . . which was exactly one dog too many! Penn lost his balance and tumbled backward, dropping all the animals.

An alarm blared through the tunnel. I needed to do something NOW.

That's when I remembered Professor Wingum's advice: The key to flying was staying balanced and steady.

I sped over to Chaos. Then I found Pax and linked their paws together.

"Hold on to one another!" I yelled as I connected more animals, paw by paw.

Soon, all the dogs were lined up, with Chaos in the front. Penn was over on the side when I shouted after him. "Hey, Penn!" I called out. "I'll push from the back. Can you help too?"

"Got it," he replied, quickly catching on to my plan.

Penn grabbed both of Chaos's paws. With all the strength I had, I pushed us ahead while Penn pulled. And we flew out of the tunnel just as the seconds on the timer went down to zero.

THE NEW MISSION

"Excellent job, Mia!" Professor Wingum cried as a bunch of kids gave me high-fives.

"Class, Mia just showed us what it takes to be a great superhero! She made a plan, acted quickly, and got everyone to safety!"

Professor Wingum gave me two big thumbs-up.

That's when it hit me. I'd been so focused on getting out of the tunnel . . . I didn't realize I was flying!

"I really *flew!*" I exclaimed happily.

"You sure did!" Wingum replied. "Your action in the face of danger helped you overcome your fears! This is known as the superhero instinct—or learning to trust yourself. All of you have it. We just teach you how to listen to it."

Chaos purred happily as she nuzzled against my leg.

"One important thing about trusting yourself is also knowing when to trust *others*, too," Wingum continued as he locked eyes with Penn. "Sometimes, even the greatest superheroes need help. Teamwork was the key to Mia *and* Penn's success."

I gave Penn a quick smile. I was so glad we made it out okay. But he just looked away!

I wondered if I had made a mistake.

"So why are there random dogs here, anyway?" Penn asked, clearly annoyed.

"Oh, they followed my cat and me from the clinic," I explained.

"Ha! Why am I not surprised?" Penn muttered under his breath.

My face grew hot as a few classmates quietly snickered. Immediately, I went from being super-proud to super-embarrassed. I may have helped solve the dog problem, but I had to admit, *I* was the one who brought the dogs in the first place.

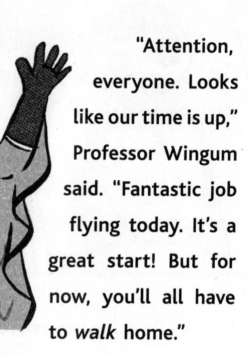

"Attention, everyone. Looks like our time is up," Professor Wingum said. "Fantastic job flying today. It's a great start! But for now, you'll all have to *walk* home."

As everyone left, Wingum motioned for Penn and me to stay behind.

"Amazing teamwork today—both of you," he cried. "But I'm afraid the job is only half done. These pooches don't belong here."

"Yes, they don't. These pups were all getting groomed for the Downtown Dog Palooza at the vet," I explained.

"Well, good thing the wind tunnel gave them these amazing blowouts!" Wingum said with a laugh.

I looked over, and he sure was right. They all looked absolutely fabulous!

"Ha! Good luck with getting those dogs back," Penn said with a smirk.

"Oh, no, Penn, you're not off the hook," Professor Wingum corrected. "Returning these pups is the new mission for *both* of you."

CHAPTER 5

CHAOS IN THE COMPASS

Penn and I walked out to the Compass in awkward silence. As I struggled to get Chaos into her carrier, I had a bad feeling this mission was doomed for failure.

Because here's the thing: A pack of rowdy animals isn't easy to control. Especially when they're super *cute*!

"Hey, Mia! You are wasting your time!" Penn yelled as I sped past him.

"But we need to get all the dogs to line up!" I cried. With Chaos's carrier still in my other hand, I rushed over to Pax, who was getting a tummy rub.

"There are just way too many distractions," Penn said.

I looked around the lobby. He was right. Rounding up these curious pups with all these superheroes walking around was going to be difficult.

"Watch and learn," Penn declared.

Then he took a deep breath and put his thumb and pointer finger up against his lips.

FWEE-OOO-WEE!

A loud high-pitched whistle echoed through the halls as a bright blue shiny dome covered the lobby. All the animals immediately sat straight up.

"Now *that* is how you get an animal's attention," Penn said matter-of-factly. "By controlling the sound waves they hear!"

I quietly watched Chaos and the dogs calmly follow Penn's voice. He may not be the easiest person to work with, but he definitely knew his stuff.

"Nice job, Penn," I said "Since the dogs always follow Chaos, I'll take the lead. You should watch from the back."

"No, *I* should go first," Penn argued. "*You* follow *us*."

Penn and I argued back and forth until the front door suddenly slid open . . . and Chaos jumped out again and dashed out the building! And just like earlier, all the dogs ran after her!

This time Penn and I *both* froze in shock.

Oh boy. Chaos was going to be the leader whether we liked it or not.

The Team Gets Bigger

By the time we ran outside, the dogs and Chaos were long gone. I paced back and forth in a panic when I heard the same noise from earlier.

Oh no! Someone was here, and the PITS door had disappeared!

I quickly hid under my cape, wishing
everything would just *freeze*.

And then . . . everything *did* freeze.

Whoa. I knew I could pause things
with my hands, but this was the first

time it worked with me just thinking about it.

I know we're in a hurry, but since things are on hold, let's back up for a second.

Remember how I said Pax's owner was my best friend?

Well, TA-DA! Here he is!

Please allow me to introduce you to Edison Stein—or Eddie for short.

I don't know what he's doing here, but I should probably unfreeze him and Penn now.

I moved my cape, and thankfully, everything unfroze. I'll really have to figure out how I did that later.

"I—I'm just looking for my . . . dog," Eddie stuttered nervously.

"Eddie, it's okay!" I said calmly. "You're right. Pax *was* here!"

All the color drained from Eddie's face.

"Who are you? How do you know me and my dog?" he asked.

I took a second to think carefully.

Other than my parents, Eddie was the only other person who knew my super-secret. But he had never seen me in my supersuit before!

"Eddie, please don't freak out. But it's me—*Mia*! Or right now, I guess I'm Mia Mayhem!"

Eddie continued to back away.

"Oh, come on. It really *is* me. I can prove it!"

Then I grabbed his hand and gave him our secret handshake. Thankfully, that made Eddie break into a smile.

"Mia—it *is* you! Your suit is SO SUPERCOOL!" he cried.

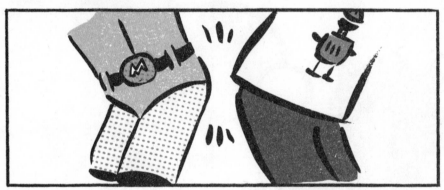

"Oh, Eddie!" I exclaimed exhaustedly. "Today has been a disaster! And we just lost a bunch of rowdy dogs . . . including Pax!"

"Well, good thing I know exactly where Pax is!" Eddie cried, holding up a tracker that he built. Eddie was really smart and always liked tinkering with things.

"Perfect!" I cried happily. "Since Pax loves other dogs, once we find him—"

"We'll find them all!" Penn piped in excitedly.

Eddie looked over his shoulder in shock. He'd been so caught off guard by me that he hadn't noticed there was another superhero right next to him!

"Very pleased to meet you, Eddie. My name is Penn Powers!" Penn said as they shook hands. "Now let's go save those pups!"

CHAPTER
7

FLYING!
OR ... SORT OF

The tracker led us to Eddie's house. We didn't know if Pax was inside, but Eddie waved at us to follow him.

"Um, Eddie," I said, "if your parents are home, we can't just walk into your house like this!"

"Oh right," he replied with a laugh. "Okay, wait here. I'll check for the dogs."

I nodded as Penn started pacing back and forth.

"Which room is Eddie's?" he asked. Penn did not like waiting around. After all, he was a superhero. And he needed to take charge.

I pointed to Eddie's open window.

"We're wasting too much time. I'm going in," Penn declared.

"No, that's really not a good idea," I said as calmly as possible.

"Don't worry. I can check this whole place in a flash!" Penn bragged. Then he took a few steps back, pushed off, and flew into Eddie's room!

UGH. Working with this kid sure wasn't easy. But now that we were a team, there was only one thing to do.

I flew through the open window and tumbled right into Eddie, who was gathering extra leashes and treats.

"Yikes!" Eddie cried. "You said you were going to wait outside!"

"Oh, I know, but *someone* was getting antsy," I said as I shot Penn a sharp look.

"Well, the dogs aren't here," said Eddie. "But I thought we could use some supplies for when we *do* find them."

"Great idea, Eddie!" I exclaimed.

Penn studied the room, and then he said, "Hey! That's a pretty good idea. What does your tracker say?"

Eddie held it up and gave it a wave. "The dogs are on the move!"

"Then so are we!" said Penn, and he flew out the window.

I shrugged. "I think he's really excited about finding the dogs."

"Yeah, I can see that," said Eddie. "I'll get my bike and meet you outside."

I flew back through the window, and a few minutes later, Eddie was out on his mountain bike.

"According to my tracker, they're headed across town!" Eddie declared.

"To cover the most area, let's split up," Penn suggested.

For once, Penn and I agreed on a plan. So we lifted into the air as Eddie raced away on his bike.

As I glided along weightlessly, I was so relieved. Flying outside was actually totally AWESOME! Especially because the horrible feeling I usually got in my stomach was gone too!

But then I looked down . . . and that big knot in my stomach came back.

The next thing I knew, I lost control and almost crashed into a bird! As I took a turn, I flew through an open

office building instead, and somehow I created a huge paper tornado! Luckily, no one saw me, and there was an exit on the other side.

But this time, there was only one place for me to go: straight into a giant tree!

"Oh, Mia! Are you okay?" Penn
asked as he rushed to my side.

I nodded as I picked leaves from my
hair. "I don't think I can do this, Penn,"
I whispered.

"Well, I think you can," he said with a smile. "Remember what we learned in class?"

"Stay balanced and steady," I replied slowly.

Penn reached down, grabbed my hands, and helped me up.

Now, here's something I wish I'd known before we left: Flying in the real world isn't the same as flying in a wind tunnel. There are a lot of unexpected things you've got to look out for. But the good news is I learned that when a friend is right next to you, even your biggest fears can disappear.

EDDIE'S WILD RIDE

Penn and I zoomed across town. The wind rushing against my face was like nothing I'd ever felt before. The knot in my stomach finally disappeared, and I was able to really look around.

We passed the post office, the movie theater, and even my favorite ice-cream shop! From up above, everything I knew so well looked completely different.

When I dove a bit lower, I saw Eddie racing down the street. He easily hopped over a curb, pedaled down a slanted pipe, and skidded past a row of trash cans.

But then he started to go down a random alley, and I knew he was in trouble. His tracker must have misled him . . . because he was heading straight into a construction site!

"Look out!" I yelled over the booming noise of giant vehicles.

Luckily, Eddie heard me just in time. He sped over a mountain of dirt, jumped a set of steel frames, and dodged a huge puddle of wet cement.

I was so relieved that Eddie was safe . . . but then I heard him scream.

"AHHHHH!" Eddie cried as a crane hook caught him!

"Don't worry, Eddie!" I yelled as I went into another dive.

I swooped down and grabbed Eddie without his bike. Then I looked over and saw that Penn had caught it.

Whew! What a close call!

I'm so glad I've gotten used to flying because it looks like even great bike riders could use a pair of superheroes.

THE FINAL DESTINATION

Back on the ground I gave Eddie a huge hug. "Maybe keep your eyes on the road next time?" I suggested.

He nodded as Penn came flying down with the bike. Right then the alarm on the tracker started going off. "Let's find these dogs already," said Penn. "I've got to get home soon. Even superheroes can't be late for dinner."

We huddled around Eddie's device and looked at the map. The red target was heading east, toward one of my favorite places in town.

"Hey! I know where they're going!" I yelled. "The park!"

It was all beginning to make sense. Remember how my cat, Chaos, was leading the pack of dogs? And remember how I said that most cats like to lay in the sun? My cat does too. But here's the thing: While most cats like to do that from a window, Chaos likes to actually lay outside.

And if she's outside, the park is her go-to place because, well, there's lots of sun, plenty of things to scratch, *and* a big playground!

Now that we had a location, it was time to get back off the ground. We decided to meet at the fountain in the park. Eddie handed us the leashes and treats.

"You'll get there before me, so I think you'll need these," he said.

Penn took the bag and nodded. "Thanks, Eddie."

Then Penn and I lifted up into the sky.

At the park, I let out a sigh of relief. Pax, Chaos, and the other dogs were really there! The park had been set up for the Downtown Dog Palooza tomorrow . . . and the dogs were running through *everything*!

They raced through tents, knocked over all the chairs, and dug through trophy boxes. I spotted one bulldog chewing on a WELCOME banner while a poodle got tangled up in a pile of streamers.

If we didn't do something fast, the dog show would be ruined!

Luckily for Penn and me, there were no people in sight. We just needed to get things under control before anyone saw us!

So we took the leashes and treats and started flying around. But as expected, a pack of hyper dogs (and a cat) is *way* too much mayhem—even for a team of two superheroes!

That's when I looked over and locked eyes with Penn. "It's time to use your special trick!" I told him.

Penn nodded and lifted two fingers to his lips.

But just as he took a deep breath, a loud whistle that sounded nothing like Penn's echoed from behind us.

CHAPTER 10

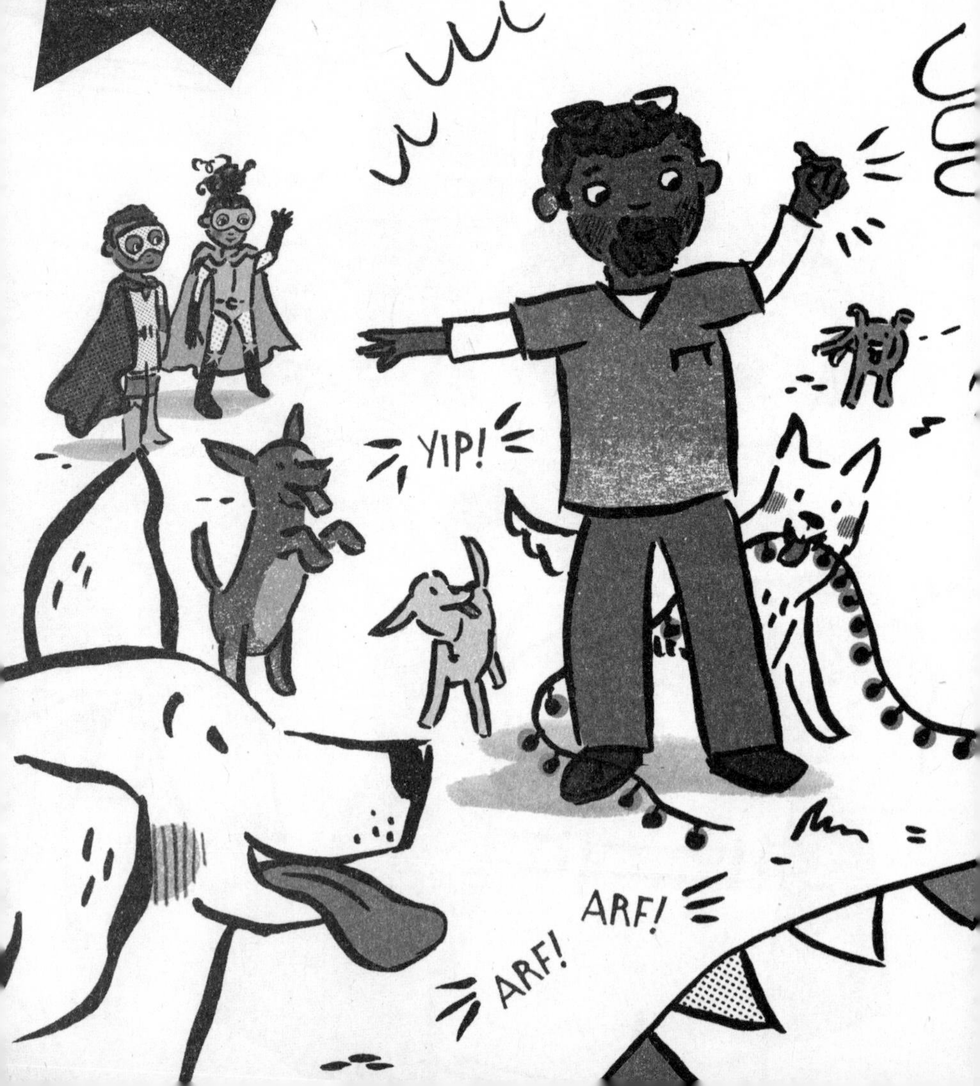

THE DREAM TEAM

When I turned around to see who it was, my jaw dropped to the floor. It was my dad! And unlike Eddie, my dad had seen me in my supersuit before, so he knew it was me.

I started to wave to Dad, but then I stopped. I realized I was in danger of breaking a major PITS superhero rule! Unless absolutely necessary, it was important to keep our secret identities under wraps. And if I wasn't careful, Penn could figure out who I was!

I looked around in a panic, but thankfully, Eddie rode up on his bike, and my dad played it cool.

"Hi, Eddie, it's good to see you," my dad said. "I have been looking for this pack of dogs all day! I never thought they would head to the park. Good thing that they're all safe."

"Well, these dogs escaped from the PI—I mean, we've been trying to get them back to you!" I said before Eddie could reply. I laughed nervously as my dad lifted an eyebrow.

Oh man. I definitely had some explaining to do when I got home.

But luckily my dad knew exactly what to say.

"Oh my goodness! Thank you for tracking them," my dad replied. "But I could use some help cleaning this up. The setup crew from the clinic already went home."

"You got it, sir!" I replied with an awkward salute. I shot Eddie a look as he struggled to hold in his laughter.

Then we split into two teams with a bunch of the dogs. Eddie and Penn fixed the chairs while my dad and I retrieved banners that had blown into the trees. Then we grabbed the streamers and secured them back onto the stage.

Once we finished, everything looked as good as new.

240

And the funny thing is that after all that mayhem, the animals were suddenly on their best behavior! So Penn and Eddie easily secured the leashes while I led Chaos inside her carrier.

After my dad secured the last dog collar, he stood up and turned to us.

"Thanks so much, Eddie, and um—" my dad began.

"Penn Powers, sir!" Penn said.

"And Mia Mayhem," I added proudly.

Then the two of us flew off as Eddie and my dad walked the dogs, and Chaos, back to the clinic.

The next day at the Downtown
Dog Palooza, I walked through all the
different stations with Chaos. There
were events for best dressed, best ball
fetcher, and even best water-skier!

When I stopped by the pool that
was set up for water-skiing, I saw that
Pax had won first place!

I opened the carrier to celebrate . . .
but Chaos had struck again!

I ran around, frantically calling her name. Thankfully, this time, I found her sleeping under a tree!

So you know how I said that most cats like taking naps? Well, I guess Chaos does too.

And before she wakes up, here are a few things I've learned: For starters, saving the day takes a lot of work. And I couldn't have done it alone.

But the good thing is, thanks to the most epic adventure across town, I, Mia Mayhem, can really FLY!

And I guess the craziest and most obvious lesson of all is that I *really* need to fix this good ole cat carrier!

VS. THE SUPER BULLY

CONTENTS

MIA MACAROONEY, THE SOCCER STAR!

Oh boy. We're totally going to lose this soccer game. I doubt we'll be able to make a comeback before time runs out. If by some miracle we do score a goal, *I* definitely need to stay out of it.

Why? Well, because the last time I was on this field, I kicked the ball so hard that I broke the goalpost by mistake!

Weird things happen to me all the time. In fact, all my life I thought I was a super-klutz. No matter how hard I tried to avoid it, I always caused a lot of mayhem.

But here's the kicker: I found out that I'm *not* a super-klutz. . . . I'm actually just SUPER!

Like for real!

I. Mia Macarooney. Am. A. Superhero!

Ever since I found out, I've had to juggle a lot. During the day, I go to Normal Elementary School. But as soon as the school bell rings, I head off to the Program for In Training Superheroes, aka the PITS. And at the PITS, I go by my superhero name, MIA MAYHEM!

My parents and my best friend are the only people who know the truth. Sometimes I wish I could tell everybody. But I've learned that keeping things quiet is the only way to protect my secret identity. My mom and dad would know best. They've been superheroes for *much* longer than me.

257

It's been a crazy ride, so I'm glad
that I still do a lot of ordinary things
like playing soccer with my friends. But
now that I'm in the middle of a losing
game, I'm starting to panic.

My best friend, Eddie, is about to
pass the ball to me!

ZIP!

Oh boy. Here
we go.

"Run, Mia! Run!"
he yells as he
throws me the ball.

So I zigzagged my way around the
other team and ran the ball all the way
down the field . . . and kicked it straight
into the goal!

By the end of the game, I scored ten goals all by myself—without even breaking a sweat!

I ran over to my teammates with the biggest grin on my face. For the first time ever, we totally beat the odds . . . thanks to me!

Now, I kind of wished everybody could have been happier for me. But for some reason, all my teammates were too tired. They didn't even care that we won!

This wasn't exactly how I hoped to finish the best game of my life, but I guess it was okay.

I've got something else to look forward to.

Today is my very first superspeed training class at the PITS.

And I have a feeling it's going to be awesome.

CHAPTER 2

MEETING ALLIE OOMPH

At the entrance to the PITS, I took out my suit. Then I spun around three times. I finally mastered the quick-superhero-change trick!

On the outside, the PITS looks like an empty, old warehouse. There's even a DO NOT ENTER sign dangling on the front. But when you walk in, it's a top secret superhero training school!

I looked around the lobby, which was known as the Compass. A group of older students walked by. I stopped a tall, slender girl in a violet suit. Maybe she would know where Dr. Dash's Fast class was.

"Oh sure!" she said, pointing to the back exit. "Fast class is outside. You need to go to the Super Cutie."

"To the super . . . *what?*" I asked, confused. But when I turned around, she was already gone.

Did she really just say "the Super Cutie"? That didn't sound right.

I walked in the direction she'd pointed, toward a big, arched door.

Maybe I needed to ask somebody else.

But then I'd have to ask if they'd seen the Super Cutie.

Um, yeah. No, thanks.

I opened the door and walked down a long tree-lined path. There was a clear, protective dome over the tall trees. Soon I saw a familiar blazing red cape up ahead.

"Hey, Penn!" I shouted excitedly, running to catch up.

When Penn Powers and I first met, we didn't exactly get off on the right foot. I thought he was a major show-off.

But luckily, we became friends after going on a flying mission to find my crazy cat.

We stood in front of a screen that looked like a robot. There were five superpower icons.

"Wow, even I've never been out here," said Penn.

I pointed at the picture that looked like three forward arrows. "Looks like Fast class is to the right," I said.

Just as we made the turn, someone knocked us down!

"Get out of the way, slowpokes!" the kid yelled, before he rushed on.

"Whoa. Are you guys okay?" asked a girl who ran over to help us up.

The girl was wearing a green
supersuit that had silver zigzags on the
elbows.

"Yeah, thanks," I replied. Then I bent
down to brush the dirt off my boots.

"Whoa—your silver leg blades are awesome!" I exclaimed, looking up. Starting from the base of the knee, each of her lower legs was made of metal. Then at the ankle, a curved blade completed each foot. They fit perfectly with her blazing green suit.

"Yeah, aren't they cool?" she asked with a grin. "I call these my Blades of Glory! I've got all different kinds of legs depending on what I'm doing.

ALLIE'S KICKS

BUNGEE BLADES

ROCKET BLADES

These ones are great for running, so it's perfect for Fast class. Are you going there too?"

I nodded, and then Penn and I introduced ourselves.

"Nice to meet you! I'm Allie Oomph," she said warmly.

Once we got to the
racetrack, there were many
kids already there . . . including the
rude kid who had knocked us over!

I wasn't too excited about that, but
I didn't have time to worry.

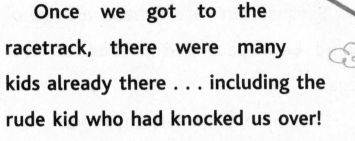

Because out of nowhere, a swirl of wind blew past and pushed us over *again*.

This time, Penn fell onto me.

I fell onto Allie.

And Allie fell onto—uh-oh. It was the rude kid.

"Hey! Get off!" the boy said as he picked himself up.

Before we could say a word, the wind stopped. Then a man with a neat mustache and a golden whistle appeared in front of us.

"Sorry! Didn't mean to knock you all over. I'm Dr. Dash—welcome to your first Fast class!"

CHAPTER 3

QT... <u>NOT</u>
CUTIE

Dr. Dash smiled. "Welcome, students. This is the hidden course called the Super Quick Track—or QT, for short."

Ha! So this is what the Super Cutie is! Penn gave me a thumbs-up.

"You will each learn how to control your speed by running around this beginner-level track," Dr. Dash continued.

The rude kid raised his hand. "This track looks *way* too easy. Can we skip ahead to a harder lesson?"

"Ah, Hugo Fast. It's good to see you," Dr. Dash replied. "The track may look easy now. But once you start running, hurdles will pop up everywhere."

POP!

Hugo didn't look happy, but he didn't argue.

"Now, let's cover the superspeed basics. Does anyone know what the most important rule is?" Dr. Dash asked.

Allie shot her hand up. "Remembering to stretch?"

"Good guess! It *is* important to relax your body." Dr. Dash smiled. "But the secret to becoming a good speedster is to take it slow and not go *too* fast. At least at first."

Everyone looked very confused.

"I know it doesn't quite make sense. But think of it this way," Dr. Dash began. "If you run several laps without preparing your body, you're going to run out of breath, right?"

Everybody nodded.

"Well, with superspeed, you can't push yourself before you're ready. If you do, you might lose your own *shadow*. And without your shadow, you'll lose your superspeed powers."

Everyone gasped, except for Hugo.

"Yes, it's very serious," Dr. Dash said. "Without your shadow, your body

will *literally* slow down. And finding a missing shadow is tricky business. Now, thankfully, there is a way to find it—but it's not something you'll need to learn now."

Whoa. Who knew your shadow could *leave* your body?

I wonder if it hurts. Well, actually, let's not think about that. I'm getting ahead of myself.

Once we finished covering the rules of speed, it was time to start a team relay race. My group included me, Penn, Allie . . . and, unfortunately, Hugo.

Each person had to run five laps while jumping over hurdles that popped up from the ground. As a penalty, every missed hurdle would be added to your team's overall time. And this combined score would be each team's final ranking for the race.

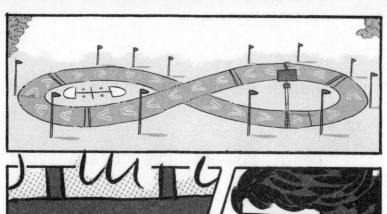

Talk about a lot of pressure, huh? But with Penn on my team, I was feeling pretty calm.

That is, until Hugo said he was taking charge. "That's the only way we'll actually place first," he insisted.

Then he tapped Penn on the shoulder to start.

"Penn Powers—I've heard your name before. Don't let me down," Hugo muttered.

Penn let out a half-hearted laugh as he and I locked eyes. Then he gave me a quick wink.

"On your marks!" Dr. Dash called out as the first group lined up. "Get set!"

Penn leaned forward, his eyes focused straight ahead.

"Go!"

Dr. Dash blew his golden whistle, and Penn sped away.

THE RELAY RACE

All the starters ran off at the speed of light. A swirling blur of color that matched each runner's supersuit filled the lane. Allie and I cheered as Penn's bright red streak zoomed around.

Penn came into focus as his first hurdle popped up from the ground. Without missing a beat, he leaped into the air.

Whoa. Did you just see that?

He made it! And now he's in the lead!

From there, the first three laps were a piece of cake. Penn easily kept a large distance between him and the other runners. And things were looking really good . . . until a loud alarm started going off.

"Oh no!" I cried. "Penn's getting tired."

"I think everyone is," said Allie.
She was right. Beeping sounds were
going off in every lane.

I watched with one eye half shut as
Penn missed five hurdles in a row.

But the good news?

Thanks to his strong start, we were still in the lead.

The problem was that now it was *my* turn.

As Penn began his last lap, I stepped up to the start line and leaned forward. My muscles tightened as Penn's red blur came closer and closer. Then he tapped me in and off I went!

An awesome tingly feeling came over me. Right then I realized that I'd felt the same amazing rush during my soccer game earlier.

Soon, I could see my first set of hurdles coming up. I took a deep breath and jumped into the air. And leaped right over them!

From there, things were a piece of cake.

Well, at least until lap three.

By then, I ran out of all my energy— just like Penn.

I watched helplessly as a pink blur zoomed by on the right. Then a green streak edged past me on the left!

In an instant, we were in danger of losing our lead!

So I looked down and pounded my feet into the ground.

But looking down was a *bad* idea because my foot got caught on a long line of hurdles. And just like that, they all fell like dominos.

Then there was *a lot* of beeping.

But I still had to tag Allie in, so I ignored it and pushed to the end.

As soon as Allie blasted off, I dropped to the floor. It felt like the whole track was spinning! Luckily, things calmed down as Penn helped me up.

I checked the board at the back of the track.

Oh boy. Somehow, we were now in last place.

And I could tell Hugo was *not* happy about it.

CHAPTER 5

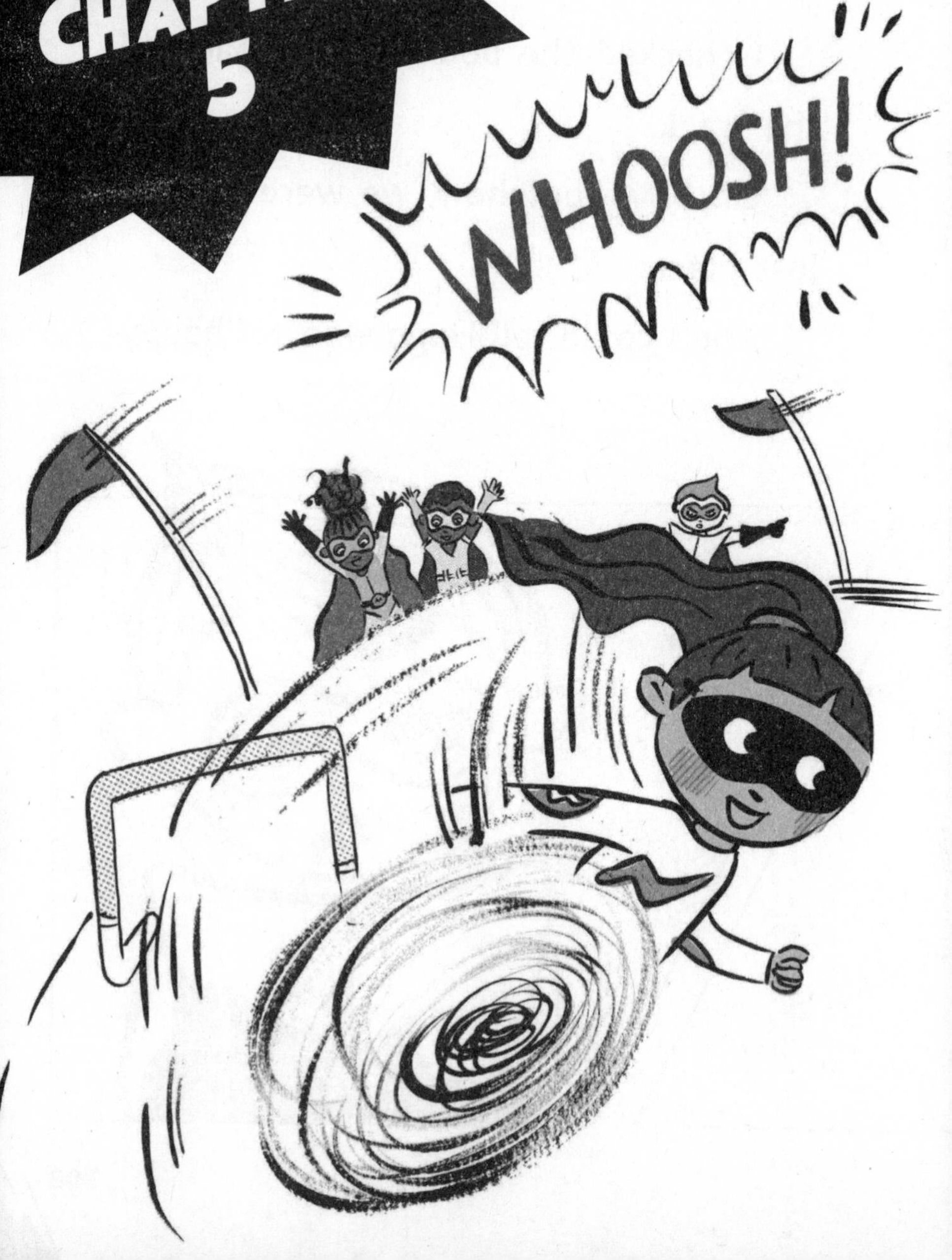

THE FINAL RESULTS

The QT race wasn't over yet, and the chances of making a comeback were slim. But Penn and I cheered at the tops of our lungs every time Allie passed by.

Hugo, on the other hand, wasn't a good cheerleader.

"Hey! You need to go faster!" he yelled as Allie came around a curve. "We're in last place!"

But Allie stayed focused and steady. Keeping her own pace.

And guess what?

It was the perfect plan.

Because by lap three, everyone else was pooped. And that's when she took her chance to get in front of a bunch of other kids.

When Allie tapped out, she was ten feet away from fourth place. She was also the only runner who hadn't missed a single hurdle!

Then it was Hugo's turn. He zoomed off in a bright orange streak.

I had to admit that as bossy as he was, he *was* a talented runner. He easily pushed forward and jumped over a string of moving hurdles.

In the end, Hugo got us up to second place.

For the first time during the whole race, I let out a sigh of relief.

"Great job, Allie! I'm so glad we made a comeback," I said.

"Thanks! I told you my blades were good for running," she replied.

"Yeah . . . well, they weren't fast enough," Hugo muttered as he walked by in a huff.

"Oh, don't listen to him," I assured her. "He's just tired."

She nodded with a bright smile.

Then Dr. Dash gathered the group. "Good job, class!" he cried. "You've finished your first race in record time.

But we need to tally up the missed
hurdles." After a long pause, he
announced the final scores. Then all
the color drained from my face.

Because we weren't in second.

We were still *last* . . . because of all the hurdles *I* missed!

"Ugh. Thanks a lot, Mia Mayhem," Hugo growled. "You undid all *my* work."

"No, it's okay, Mia," Allie said, patting me on the back. "This was a team effort. It's not your fault."

"Well, *you* ran like a slowpoke too. Never mind your Blades of Glory. They're more like Blades of GRASS!" Hugo shot back.

"Ha! Well, actually my blades are made of metal. But maybe I should put green stripes on them! They'd match my suit," Allie replied with a big grin.

But Hugo tried again.

"Oh, that won't help. Because blades of grass *can't run*," Hugo said. "Like you."

Allie's smile didn't waver. But I decided enough was enough.

"You know what, Hugo?" I said, jumping in. "Allie is not the problem. You are."

"No, I'm not. I'm the only one who actually *helped* the team. Even Penn messed up," he said, crossing his arms.

"Well, you sure aren't acting like a team member. Putting the blame on us just makes you a sore loser," I said.

"What did you say?" he asked as he got closer.

Penn tried to step in. But nothing was going to scare me—

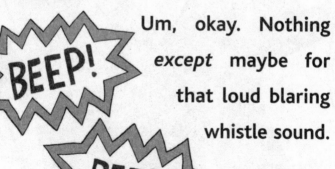

Um, okay. Nothing *except* maybe for that loud blaring whistle sound.

THE LOST SHADOW

"Great job today, everyone!" Dr. Dash cried. "Class is dismissed. Make sure to get lots of rest for next week."

As the other kids left, I thought Hugo would make another snarky comeback. But I guess my plan worked because he just walked away.

"Don't worry about him," I said, turning to Allie.

"Oh, yeah, he doesn't bother me," she said. "He's just in a bad mood."

"Yeah, and it might never change," I said as we all laughed.

Then Penn, Allie, and I started the walk back to the PITS building. That's when another dizzy spell hit me. I steadied myself against a tree.

"What's wrong, Mia?" Penn asked as he came over.

"I don't know. I'm just a little dizzy," I replied.

"Oh no!" Dr. Dash suddenly chimed in from behind. "Mia, can I please see you for a moment? It won't take long."

So my friends left, and I followed Dr. Dash back to the track.

"Mia, would you please stand in sunlight?" he asked.

"Sure," I said as I walked out of the shade. My legs suddenly felt heavy.

"Oh, Mia," he said slowly. "I'm afraid what I'd warned about earlier has happened. You pushed your body too hard, and now your shadow is gone."

What? He couldn't be serious.

But I looked behind me . . . and he was right! My shadow had vamoosed!

"Oh no! It really is gone! Does that mean I've lost my superpowers?" I asked.

"Yes, your superspeed powers are gone," Dr. Dash said. "So your body will start to slow down. But don't worry."

"Are you sure?" I asked, trying to keep my voice steady.

"Yes, we'll have to start a special search, and—" he began.

But then a loud sound made us both jump.

Dr. Dash pulled his phone out of his pocket.

"Er—excuse me, Mia. This is a call I *have* to take."

So I waited patiently under a tree. And when he came back, he looked really worried.

"Sorry. Where was I?" he asked as he scratched his eyebrow. "Being shadowless *will* be uncomfortable, but you just need to be careful," he said. "The bad news is that we have to put the search on hold. I've been called into a secret runaway-train operation!"

Okay, hold on. Did you hear that?

I know I'm in quite a pickle myself. But a runaway train? Now that I'm a superhero, I know an emergency when I hear one. So we agreed to put the search on hold, and I headed back to the PITS. Really slowly.

When I finally made it inside, Penn

and Allie were waiting for me. So I
told them my shadow was missing, but
Dr. Dash would help after taking care
of a secret mission. Now, I wasn't too
worried about the waiting . . . until a
random note fell out of my locker.

It said:

Meet me on the QT in two days, if you DARE. One more race. Just you and me.

-HF

Oh boy. I don't know what I just walked into. But I have a feeling I should have never called Hugo a sore loser.

CHAPTER 7

THE BAD LUCK DAY

At regular school the next morning, I was back on the soccer field. But today, I was moving super-slowly and was in no mood to play.

"Oh no. Looks like it's going to rain, huh?" Eddie asked.

"Uh, yeah. Thanks, Captain Obvious," I shot back.

Okay. So I didn't mean to be rude.

But I didn't want
to think about
the weather.

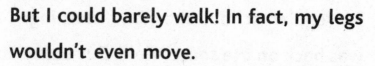

When the
whistle blew, I
ran toward the ball.
But I could barely walk! In fact, my legs
wouldn't even move.

So, unlike last time, I was *not*
Mia, the soccer star. I was Mia, the
benchwarmer, who
couldn't play.

After the game,
Eddie came over to
check on me.

But I couldn't tell him that I'd lost my shadow. It was too risky that others could hear. And I had

bigger problems on my mind. So as soon as the bell rang, I left without saying good-bye.

At the PITS, I ran
into the one person
I didn't want to see.
Hugo Fast was standing in the middle
of the Compass. If he knew that I really
was a slowpoke now, he'd use it against
me. So I slowly turned around to leave.
But I bumped right into Allie and Penn
and landed right on my butt!

As my friends helped me up, I told them my plan. I couldn't wait for Dr. Dash. The search had to start now.

And since a team was faster than doing it alone, we decided to split up outside. Penn flew over the trees but found nothing, while Allie turned over heavy, fallen tree trunks.

As for me? I had no choice but to trail behind. And tell them where to look.

"Hey, Mia! I found something!" Allie called out excitedly.

Please, please, please be my shadow, I thought.

She was pointing to a big black circle on the ground.

I inched closer and poked it with my fingers. It was wet and super-shiny.

"Ugh. Since when do I look like a puddle?" I snapped as I fell in.

I knew Allie and Penn were trying to help. But this search was a total bust.

And I was now officially out of time.

At dinner that night, I told my parents about my day full of bad luck. My friends didn't understand, but my mom and dad would see it from my side. Or at least I thought they would.

"You have a bigger problem than your missing shadow," my mom said.

I looked at her, totally not following.

"Mia, losing your shadow makes things hard. But it'll come back," my dad explained.

My mom nodded. "I know there's a lot going on, but it sounds like you've been pretty mean. Always remember that it's hard to find good friends."

CHAPTER
8

SLOW AND STEADY

The next morning was another gray and gloomy day. After the last PITS dismissal bell, I was stretching on the QT when Hugo showed up.

"Wow, so you came," Hugo said. "I thought you would chicken out."

"No, I'm not a chicken," I replied.

"And *I* don't like being called a sore loser," Hugo snapped back.

So I actually *was* pretty nervous. But I needed to act cool. I wiped my sweaty hands at my sides.

"All right," Hugo said. "On my count, we're going to do twenty laps."

"What? Twenty laps!" I cried.

If I'd failed at five laps, how was I going to do twenty?

"Running the team relay race by ourselves is the only way to see who the real winner is," Hugo said with a smirk.

Now I really wanted to run away. But I knew I *literally* couldn't escape.

So there was only one option: I had to run the race . . . even if I lost horribly.

I took a deep breath and looked ahead. But then two figures flew down and landed right in front of us!

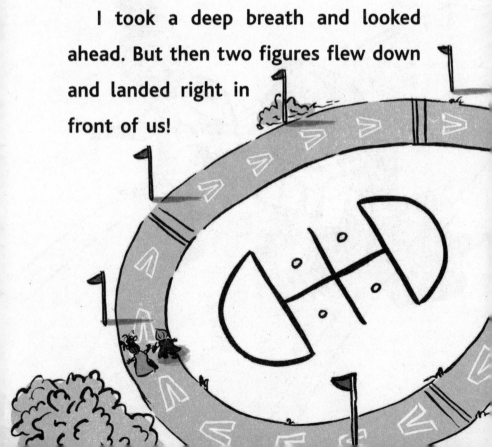

It was Allie and Penn. With pom-poms!

They gave me a wink and then ran over to the sidelines as Hugo started counting down.

ZOOM!

"Three . . . two . . . one. GO!" he yelled.

And just like that, the race was on. Hugo passed me five times before I even finished the first lap. I was going *super*-slow, but sweat still dripped down my face. I didn't even have blue-and-yellow sparks behind me! So I was feeling pretty down as I started my third lap.

"Mia, stay focused and steady!" Penn yelled from the sidelines.

"Yeah, and keep the pace!" Allie added.

Hearing her voice calmed me down. During the team race, Allie hadn't let Hugo bully her into going fast. And like Dr. Dash had said, pacing was the secret to superspeed!

I smiled and gave Allie a thumbs-up.

I was finally ready to finish this—whether I lost or not.

CHAPTER
9

CONNECTING THE PIECES

I was ten laps in when I realized it was starting to get easier.

I had no idea why. But like Dr. Dash told us, building speed was most important. Maybe while I was walking in the woods yesterday, I'd actually been preparing for today!

Whatever it was, I was definitely feeling better.

I felt a burst of speed and glanced behind me. The yellow and blue sparks were starting to come back!

As I rounded a curve, that's when I saw it.

A weird-shaped black blob was trailing behind me.

It looked like a person's hand . . . and then I realized it was a piece of my shadow!

I looked up at the sky. The big, dark clouds had finally parted. With the sunlight in my face, I kept on running as the black blob got bigger and bigger. Soon my full shadow was following behind me! I clenched my fists and realized they were totally dry. Who knew your shadow helped you from getting gross and sweaty!

With my body back up to speed, I easily sped around the track nine more times. Then finally, it was my last lap. I was trailing behind Hugo by just a few feet. I pushed as hard as I could, but Hugo passed the finish line first.

So, in the end, I lost again. But it was okay. I still felt great.

"Congratulations, Hugo," I said, catching my breath. "And I'm sorry I called you a sore loser."

"Yeah, whatever. But this time, I won fair and square," he said.

I nodded. Then Penn and Allie joined me, and Hugo left for the PITS.

"Oh, Mia, what a great race!" said a voice from behind.

I turned around and saw Dr. Dash.

"Sorry we couldn't find your shadow together, but it looks like you didn't need me!"

"It's because my friends helped me remember what was most important," I said, turning to Allie and Penn.

Then we all high-fived. And our shadows did too!

"One more thing," I said. "Sorry about snapping at you before. I was worried about finding my shadow, but that's no excuse for being a bad friend."

"That's okay," Penn said.

"Yeah, we understand," Allie said.

"Thanks, guys. You're the best," I said with a big smile. "But now that this race is over . . . the last one back to the PITS is a total slowpoke!"

CHAPTER 10

THE FINAL RACE

By the time we had our next class with Dr. Dash, I'd secretly been racing everywhere.

And good thing, too, because our next class was harder.

"All right, students! Today we're taking it to the next level! We'll have hurdles like before, but they will have an extra surprise."

Then he pushed a few buttons on his wristband. And all of a sudden, a whole group of superhero teachers landed in front of us, each with a brightly colored ball. One of the balls burst as Dr. Sue Perb landed, spraying water everywhere!

Oh boy. Giant water balloons!

"You'll also have to look out for us!" Dr. Dash cried excitedly. "Everybody, ready?"

Half of us cheered. Half of us groaned. And I was totally ready.

We were put into the same teams from before. As expected, Hugo wanted to take charge. And that was fine with me as long as I had my shadow.

Dr. Dash blew his whistle and soon, Allie was off! She wasn't the fastest, but she was steady and jumped over every hurdle and balloon!

Penn went second. He had trouble with the same hurdles as last time, but he still got us into first place.

Then it was my turn.

I started slowly, making sure I wasn't pushing too hard. Luckily, I was feeling strong, so I picked up speed. In the end, I avoided every single obstacle!

Then, like before, Hugo was the last runner on our team. His speed was good, but he couldn't focus on the hurdles and the balloons at the same time—so almost every single water balloon hit him. By the time he finished his final lap, he was soaking wet.

"Okay," Dr. Dash said at the end. "Time to calculate the number of missed hurdles per team."

We all held our breath and waited.

"Congratulations! The team in first place is Allie, Penn, Mia, and Hugo!"

Allie tapped me on the back. "This is because of you! You ran so well and avoided every single hurdle!"

"Oh, it was a team effort!" I said. "And also, I actually owe a lot to Hugo. If he hadn't dared me to race him again the other day, I never would have done so well!"

Hugo just scowled as a trail of water followed behind him. "You just had some good luck today," he said. Then he walked away in a huff.

And you know what? He was right. I *was* lucky. But not the way he thought.

I was lucky to have great friends.

And I was even luckier that those friends knew how to be a good friend to me, even when I wasn't. Because after all, true friends support one another, even on the gloomiest of days. Just like Penn, Allie, and my best friend, Eddie.

That's when I realized I wasn't done with my apologies. I still owed one to him for being rude during our last soccer game!

There was so much to explain, and this apology couldn't wait for a single extra second.

But thank goodness I now know how to run superfast.

BZzz!

My room is a mess. I'm digging around in my closet because I've ripped another shoelace.

This is the fifth one I've ripped in two days. The *fifth*! For some reason, they keep tearing in half when I try to pull the bunny ears through the loop.

Don't ask me why. The only answer I've got is this: Disasters, even tiny little shoelace-size disasters, follow me around everywhere.

They happen during the day at regular school. And they also happen *after* school, at the Program for In Training Superheroes, aka the PITS. That's the top secret training academy where I learn how to use my superpowers!

Yeah, you heard me right.

My name is Mia Macarooney, and I. Am. A. Superhero!

But at the PITS, I go by Mia Mayhem.

And guess what? So far, I've learned how to fly *and* run with superspeed.

But here's the thing: Even superheroes sometimes have shoelace trouble.

So that's why there was a huge mess on my floor when my mom walked into my room.

Excerpt from *Breaks Down Walls*

"Hey, sweetie. There's something I want to give you," she said as she sat down.

"Is it a new shoelace?" I asked.

"No, it's *way* better than a shoelace," she replied.

Then she held out a small box.

I took it from her hand and opened it. Inside, on top of a tiny cushion, was a shiny star pendant with a single blue stone in the middle, and lightning bolts on either side. It was the coolest necklace I'd ever seen.

"Wow, this is *so* cool!" I cried. "Is it my birthday today?"

"Ha! No, it isn't," she said, smiling. "But I know how hard you've been working lately. Going to regular school *and* juggling PITS training is a lot."

I nodded. It *was* a lot sometimes.

"Your grandma gave this to me after *I* started training at the PITS. This was her necklace when *she* was a girl, and I think you're ready to have it. It's a family good luck charm!"

Good luck charm? Perfect. I needed all the luck I could get right now.

I thanked my mom and gave her a huge hug before she left.

Then I took a better look at the

necklace. It was the perfect shade of blue and would even go with my suit.

It was so pretty that I couldn't stop staring at it.

But then I had to. Because my cat suddenly jumped up, pushed me down, and started licking me like crazy before running off.

"Oh, Chaos! I can't play right now!" I told her, sitting back up.

I love my cat, but sometimes she is a handful. Even for me.

I opened my hands to put the necklace on.

But then my stomach dropped.

Excerpt from *Breaks Down Walls*

My hands were empty.

I got up and did a quick scan of the floor. Then I checked all my pockets, took off my socks, and even looked inside my dirty old shoe.

But the necklace was gone!

I'd been distracted for only *one minute*. That's it. *One minute!*

But somehow, a tiny shoelace disaster had become an epic missing necklace search.

"Hey, Chaos!" I yelled, totally panicked. "Where is my necklace?"

Excerpt from *Breaks Down Walls*

I got down on my knees and looked at her face-to-face.

"You hid the necklace, didn't you? Just so I'd play?"

She gave no response. But trust me. I know a cat smirk when I see one.

And the necklace *had* to be somewhere in my room. I just needed to know where to look.

I threw my favorite cat pillow off my bed.

Nope, not there.

So I picked up the bed itself and peeked under.

Lots of dust bunnies, but nope . . . not there either.

So next, I dumped all the dirty clothes out of my hamper.

Lots of smelly clothes, but again, no necklace.

Right then, as if on cue, Chaos dragged a pair of dirty pants across the floor, while wearing one of my socks!

Now usually, I'd run around chasing her . . . and make an even bigger mess.

But today, I really didn't have time. So I stayed focused and kept searching.

I lifted up my dresser with one hand and checked under there.

Then I tossed it next to my dirty clothes.

Then I threw my chair on top.

Then my desk.

Then my bookcase, too.

Before I knew it, everything was stacked on top of one another.

But I still had *no* necklace.

Oh boy.

What was I supposed to tell my mom?

I looked up and saw Chaos lying on top of the bookcase near the ceiling. And that's when I remembered: I'd been too busy looking *under* my stuff that I forgot that Chaos actually loves climbing to the very top of things . . . even if she can't get back down.

My parents don't usually use their powers inside the house.

So I'm guessing I shouldn't either. But *this* was an emergency.

I flew to the top of the bookcase and grabbed Chaos with both hands.

And that's when I saw it: The shiny star necklace was around her neck, hanging right in front of me this whole time.

Now, don't ask me how she got the necklace on. I have no idea. But it doesn't matter. I finally found it!

Excerpt from *Breaks Down Walls*

When we were back on the floor, I took the necklace from Chaos. Then I put it back inside the tiny jewelry box. After all that mayhem, I definitely was *not* going to wear it today.

I tucked the box safely underneath my blanket and then looked around. My room was a total disaster.

Hopefully, my mom wouldn't notice because this mess would have to wait.

Right now, it was time for Power Hour at the PITS!